All of My Heart

SHERRY KYLE

"Love is patient, love is kind. It does not envy, it does not boast, it is not proud. It does not dishonor others, it is not self-seeking, it is not easily angered, it keeps no record of wrongs."
~ 1 Corinthians 13:4-5

CHAPTER ONE

S ierra Jacobs dug her gloved hands into the rich California soil to plant the last of the lemon trees for Napa Valley's Farmhouse Inn. Three flat acres of organic farm-style gardens was no easy feat, but it was her job to make the fruit and vegetable gardens spectacular and unique for the farm-to-table bed and breakfast.

The sun shone bright overhead, and Sierra swiped the back of her gloved hand across her damp brow. Even though the temperature was a comfortable sixty-seven degrees, she'd worked up a sweat.

For the past three weeks, she'd been sleeping on a custom French-styled bed upholstered in Belgian linen. At the end of each day, she'd crashed the second she laid her head on the pillow. Owners Trish and Ed Brown, a couple in their fifties, had renovated the 1860s farmhouse with luxurious bedrooms and bathrooms, fireplaces and private decks, and they treated their guests, even those they hired, with exceptional care.

Trish approached now and handed her a glass. "Thought you'd like some iced tea."

"You're a lifesaver." Sierra brought the chilled glass to her lips and took several big gulps. "Thank you. This is delicious."

Trish smiled. "Most people love my peach tea."

Sierra downed the rest and gave the glass back to Trish. "Thank you."

"You work too hard," Trish said. "Feel free to get out of the sun for a bit and cool yourself down on the porch."

She shook her head. "With these muddy shoes? I wouldn't think of it."

Trish folded her arms across her slender frame. "I wouldn't live out in the country if I was afraid of a little dirt."

Sierra didn't need to be asked twice. "Well, then, I'll take you up on your offer."

"Follow me." Trish took the lead. "I baked persimmon cookies this morning. I'll bring you some. I need to keep my gardener happy."

True, she worked with plants and was a horticulturist by trade, but she'd made it clear in the contract that it was up to Trish and Ed to find a permanent gardener. Her job was to create the gardens, but it was up to each inn or restaurant owner to hire someone to care for the plants. Her business was named Plant and Go for a reason: She planted gardens and left.

Thanks to her grandmother, she knew what herbs, vegetables, and fruit to plant to create amazing cuisine. And just like Betty Jacobs, Sierra enjoyed cooking more than gardening.

Once they reached the porch, Trish gestured for her to take a seat in one of the rocking chairs. "I'll be right back." She set Sierra's glass on a side table and went inside the house, the screen door slapping against its wood frame.

Sierra sat in the closest rocking chair, leaned her head back, and closed her eyes. She took in some deep calming breaths. Trish was right. It felt good to get out of the sun and take a break.

A few minutes later, Trish placed a white pitcher on the small side table, along with a vintage plate. Three delicious-looking cookies sat on top. "Here you go. I brought more tea."

"Thank you," Sierra said.

"Just looking out for you is all." Trish smiled, but her grin quickly faded. "I'm going to miss you. Are you sure you have to leave?"

This part of Sierra's business was always tricky. After spending so much time with the owners, they'd become close, and leaving was difficult. But as beautiful as the valley was with its rolling countryside and vibrant colors, she was ready to move on to her next job—creating a garden for a new farm-to-table restaurant in Palm Springs.

She pulled off her work gloves and took a cookie from the plate. "I'm going to miss you too. Your inn is beautiful, and I love it here, but I have another garden to plant. Tasty Eats and Treats is expecting me next week." As long as their recent kitchen fire didn't close their establishment for good. She took a bite of persimmon cookie.

Trish pressed her lips together. "Hiring a permanent gardener has been difficult. Is there nothing I can do to keep you here? The last thing we want to do is ruin your beautiful garden. Besides, I have a feeling you and my son would really hit it off."

It wasn't the first time one of her clients had tried to set her up. "I appreciate the invitation, but I know you'll do just fine." She gave her what she hoped was a reassuring smile.

"I understand you have another job." Trish fiddled with the edge of her cotton blouse. "I'll leave you to enjoy your break."

Once again, Trish slipped inside the farmhouse.

At moments like this, Sierra wondered how long she could travel from place to place and town to town. Most times she felt like a nomad, but she'd chosen this lifestyle when she started Plant and Go.

During college, she'd never considered she would actually start the company that began as a fun project in her business class, but when she'd had the rift with her father, and then the texts and phone calls from Eric stopped coming, it seemed as good a time as any. Plant and Go became her way out of Dove Creek.

However, she'd quickly discovered throughout her travels that there was no place like the sleepy little town in the heart of the Great Smoky Mountains.

And she missed it.

She ate the rest of the persimmon cookie and grabbed another, then put on her gloves and went out to the garden and planted the last lemon tree.

A ping sounded from her back pocket.

She pulled out her phone and looked at the text. It was Dad.

Accident. Call me.

Her heart pounded. Was this a ruse to get her attention? The silly question dissipated the second it entered her mind. Her dad wouldn't have contacted her unless it were important. She tapped in her dad's number.

The phone rang once.

"Sierra, thank you for calling. Grandma fell and broke her wrist. She's in surgery now. I know we haven't been on the best of terms lately, but can you come home? I could really use your help."

Poor Grandma. She was always the picture of health. But to go home to Dove Creek?

Flashes of her last conversation with her dad ran through her mind. She'd said some nasty things. Then again, her dad blamed her for things that weren't her fault.

Her thoughts shifted.

How would her father be able to run Camp Jacobs without Grandma? They were a team, her dad organizing the events and her grandma supplying the meals.

Her mind played tug-of-war with her emotions. Yes, she missed home, but the issue between her and her dad hadn't been resolved. How could she go home with words still left unsaid?

Yet how could she stay away when her grandma needed her?

"Sierra? You there?" Dad asked.

She blew out a puff of air, her decision made. "Should I fly or drive?"

"Our guests won't arrive until next week..."

Personally, she needed her truck and the driving time to gather her thoughts. "Then I'll see you in a few days." She'd let the owner of Tasty Eats and Treats know of her sudden change of plans on the drive to Dove Creek.

"Great! Thank you. See you then." Was that a hint of a smile in his tone?

She quickly pushed down the lump in her throat as she ended the call and tucked the cell phone into her back pocket.

At least her exit would be swift when she packed up her suitcase and said goodbye to Trish and Ed. She had somewhere she needed to be, even if she was going back to the small town that had broken her heart, not once but twice.

Thank goodness she'd only need to face her father. Seeing Eric Holden would be an entirely different matter.

Good thing he didn't live in Dove Creek.

CHAPTER TWO

After the last of his patients left the building, Dr. Eric Holden locked the door and went inside his office to call Pigeon Forge Hospital to find out how Betty Jacobs was coping after her recent fall and surgery.

He and Kevin Jacobs, Sierra's dad, had been the first on the scene. They'd been in the middle of a meeting when they'd heard the commotion. Poor woman had been on the floor, writhing in pain and clutching her badly deformed wrist.

The hospital receptionist transferred his call to Betty's room.

"Hello. Betty here."

Eric smiled. "You sound energetic."

"That's because I go home tomorrow. One more night until I sleep in my own bed."

"That's great," he said. "How's the wrist?"

"In a cast," she quipped.

"Well, that's good." He chuckled. "Seriously, though, I want you to take it easy. You have more energy than most women your age, and I know it will take a lot to keep you resting."

"Spoken like a doctor," she said. "How's your practice? I hear you've had some nagging Nellies. I don't know why, but some people have a hard time making a transition."

"Doc Walters is a hard act to follow."

"Yes, well, people loved and trusted Doctor Walters for over forty years," she said. "Give it time. Soon they will love and trust you too."

"Thanks for the vote of confidence," he said. "It's been hard being the new kid on the block."

"Hang in there," she said. "Change is difficult."

"Doc Walters is stepping in for me next week. That should make the community happy, assuming I'm still needed at Camp Jacobs. Haven't had a chance to talk with Kevin about whether the guests are still coming. I figured with you being out of commission, it might be cancelled."

"Cancelled? Oh no. You don't know my son. If there is a chance for income, he always figures out a way."

"That's good. But without you, Camp Jacobs will need a cook. Did he hire someone?"

"Hire?" Betty's tone shot up. "You haven't heard?"

He sat back in his chair. "I wouldn't ask if I had."

"Sierra's coming home." Betty's excitement was palpable. "In fact, she might be there now."

Sierra.

He sat up straight. He had hoped she'd return, had wanted it since the day he arrived in Dove Creek four months ago.

He had met Sierra at camp the summer before his senior year of high school. They'd connected over their love of good food, music, and the Great Smoky Mountains. Throughout that week of camp, they'd laughed, flirted, and by the end, exchanged phone numbers. Afterward, texts and phone calls flowed back and forth, until one day they stopped. He blamed it on medical school—and a broken promise. He'd kicked himself for not making good on visiting Sierra in college. His lame excuse of needing to study only pulled them farther apart. More times than he dared to admit, he wished he could go back and make sure he'd kept up the relationship. They'd been close, and as he neared the end of his residency, he'd longed to reconnect.

When the head of his residency mentioned that his mentor and friend was about to retire from his practice in the small town of Dove Creek, it seemed like fate. Eric jumped at the chance to become the new town doctor. He couldn't wait to practice medicine, but he was even more excited to finally get the chance to see Sierra again.

But she was gone.

Then three weeks ago he discovered Sierra had been planting a garden at Napa Valley's Farmhouse Inn. He had seriously considered booking a flight, but seeing her again at Camp Jacobs was by far the better plan—for memories' sake and his new job.

"Eric? Dr. Holden, did you hear me?" Betty's question brought him out of his reverie.

"I did." The words sounded more confident than he felt.

"Wonderful. I'm sure you'll be more than happy to spend the week with her at Camp Jacobs." She yawned. "I'd better get some shuteye before dinner arrives."

"Good idea. Rest while you can. Take care, Betty. And if you need a ride home tomorrow, please let me know."

"Thank you, dear. You're the best. Good night."

He hung up the phone and sat back in his desk chair, still in awe that Sierra was coming back to Camp Jacobs. He'd hoped she would return, but never imagined the day would finally come.

The front doorbell rang.

He glanced at the clock. Six p.m. Doc Walters was punctual. Eric went to the front door and opened it.

"Ready for our monthly meeting?" the white-haired man asked, his mustache twitching.

"Yes. Please come in." Eric offered to hang up Doc Walters's coat on the rack, and he led him into his office. It still felt strange to be the man in charge and sit behind the large desk, leaving Doc Walters to take a seat in the smaller chair in front of him.

"Have any tough cases recently?" Doc asked, jumping right in.

"A case of shingles, anaphylactic shock due to a bee sting, strep throat, and the like. Nothing I can't handle," he said, his tone even.

"Wonderful." Doc Walters leaned back in his chair. "What about pregnancies? Have any of those?"

He shook his head. "Not one case."

Doc Walters furrowed his brows. "That's what I was afraid of."

"I know there are young couples in this town. I just figured there was a lull—"

"There's never a lull when it comes to babies," Doc said. "In fact, I've had several calls just this week. Apparently pregnant women in Dove Creek don't feel comfortable seeing a new doctor. They want experience. I hate to tell you this, but they've been going to Pigeon Forge for medical care."

"Pigeon Forge, really? When they have a highly capable doctor right here?" He sat up straight and puffed out his chest, attempting to give the illusion of confidence.

"That's what I've been telling them when they call, but nonetheless they feel more comfortable going to a seasoned doctor."

Beside those pregnant women, were there others who drove the thirty-five miles to Pigeon Forge? Eric massaged a temple.

"I've come to a conclusion that you might not like." Doc Walters's words interrupted Eric's downward spiral.

He winced. "Am I fired?"

"Fired? No, son." He shook his head. "But instead of me taking over your practice for the week while you're at Camp Jacobs, I will go to camp and you will stay here."

His week with Sierra was slipping through his fingers. "But why?"

"As you know, all the camp guests will be pregnant. They will be more comfortable with a doctor who's been practicing for a long time."

As much as he hated to admit it, Doc Walters was right. Kevin and Betty had planned a week of pampering for expectant couples, otherwise known as a babymoon, and what better way for the guests to stay calm than to have a seasoned doctor around?

"I see your point, but I am a licensed doctor and have had plenty of OB experience..." As the words came out, he checked his motives. Which did he want more? To help the expectant couples or to reunite with Sierra? The answer was definitely both.

"Eric, I've already spoken with Kevin Jacobs. He agrees. I'm sorry if this is uncomfortable for you."

Suddenly this felt like a competition.

Was Doc Walters having regrets about retiring? Or was this about ego and his need for affirmation? Or maybe Doc Walters was shooting straight and Eric simply wasn't the man for the job. After all the years in training, it felt like a knife to the gut. Betty's words from their phone conversation ran through his mind.

"People loved and trusted Doctor Walters for over forty years. Give it time. Soon they will love and trust you too."

Apparently not soon enough.

He released a breath. "I guess that's it then. Have a good week at camp. Be careful, there're a lot of hills."

"Kevin has already thought about that. He has golf carts for me and the guests."

"Sierra's father has thought of everything—"

"Except one. It would be nice to have another set of capable hands with me if anyone goes into labor. Can I count on you?"

Eric nodded emphatically. "You know you can."

"Great," Doc said. "I'll let Kevin know he'll have two doctors on board if the need arises. If there's nothing else you'd like to discuss, I'll be on my way."

"Nothing I can think of, sir." The lifelong etiquette slipped off his tongue.

"Great." Doc Walters glanced at the papers strewn about Eric's desk. "I see you still have work to do. I'll let myself out."

The older man got up, his expression a bit strained as he stood, and walked out of his office, albeit slowly, toward the front door. Maybe Eric's concern about how the doctor would manage had been warranted.

Once he heard the click of the door's handle, he finished his paperwork, removed his white coat, and headed upstairs to his apartment. The 1837 Victorian was both his home and office, and came with the practice. Not only had Dr. Walters retired from doctoring, but he and his wife had given up their living quarters as well, which would be a hard move for anyone. Both were going through change. And change, no matter what, was difficult.

The hardwood floor creaked as he climbed the stairs and entered his apartment. Before he arrived in Dove Creek, the people of the town had pitched in to renovate the place. It was a nice gesture. But after today's meeting with Doc Walters, it was apparent he had yet to prove himself a competent doctor in this town.

Simon rubbed against his leg to greet him.

Eric leaned over, picked up the black and white cat, and gave him a gentle rub. "Miss me, buddy?" He set Simon on the kitchen island, opened a can of cat food, and scooped it into his bowl.

Eric's stomach growled. He hadn't eaten since noon, seven hours earlier. "I'm hungry too."

He opened his refrigerator, pulled out leftover meatloaf, and placed it in the microwave to heat. He grasped silverware and a bottle of Perrier, and brought his dinner to the couch to watch *Frasier* reruns.

His cell phone pinged and he reached for it.

Hey Eric! Guess who will be coming to Camp Jacobs next week? Me! That makes David happy because, as you know, he won't be there. Duty calls! I'm used to it. That's life in the military. I'm looking forward to catching up with you. And if I need a partner for any of the activities, I know I can count on you. Alyssa.

How could he break it to his sister-in-law that he wouldn't be there? It sounded as if Alyssa was counting on him to take care of her. It didn't surprise him. She'd been through several rounds of fertility treatments to get pregnant with this baby.

He texted her back, using words to describe Dr. Walters like "best possible care," "experience," and "everyone loves and trusts him." Apparently, pregnant women relied on doctors with years of practice delivering babies, not newbies just out of training.

"But Pigeon Forge? Really, Lord?" That news had brought down his self-esteem a few notches.

No, he wouldn't be at Camp Jacobs, but that didn't change the fact that Sierra was coming back to Dove Creek. And if he brought Betty home from the hospital, there was a good chance he would see Sierra tomorrow.

A smile tugged at his lips.

He couldn't wait.

CHAPTER THREE

The open driver's side window allowed the spring breeze to filter through Sierra's truck, the rich, fragrant scent of sweet pinesap lingering in the air like a cloud of perfume. There wasn't another smell quite like it.

The sign for Dove Creek came into view, and her breath hitched. She hadn't seen that sign since she'd glanced at it in her rearview mirror, her heart torn and tires squealing. How could her father blame her for her mother's death? True, he'd never said those exact words, but the implication was crystal clear.

"If only you had come to get me," he'd said.

If only.

Since she'd left town, her grandma had told her countless times that no amount of CPR would've saved her mom. She'd died from an undetected congenital heart defect. Didn't her father understand that? How could he put that responsibility on her?

She pushed down her emotions as she drove down Ash Street. The main street was lined with small shops and restaurants. As she passed Darlene's Country Kitchen, her mouth watered for some of Darlene's country ham, Memphis ribs, and moon pie, followed by a glass of her famous sweet tea.

She craned her neck to see a glimpse of the beautiful Victorian building where she was prescribed medication when she fell ill, had annual physicals, and where she'd received stitches in her forehead after a spill on her bicycle. Dr. Walters was a constant in this town, and he gave comfort to all who needed it.

Oddly, a small black sedan sat in the driveway. Ever since Doc's wife had given him a Buick, he'd driven nothing else. Had something happened to him? The thought brought a pang to her chest.

What else had changed in Dove Creek since she'd left?

A mile into town, she spotted the sign for Camp Jacobs. The brightly painted letters tugged at the corners of her mouth, her smile widening at the sweet memory of painting it with Eric. But just as quickly, her grin fell. Without an explanation for the abrupt end to their relationship, the only conclusion she could come up with was that he'd found someone new while attending medical school. Over the past year the sting of the rejection had lessened a bit, but the drive back to Dove Creek brought all of the memories flooding back.

She turned into the camp's driveway. The truck's tires crunched on the dirt and gravel road. Her heart beat a strange rhythm as she inched closer to the main part of camp—and the reunion with her dad.

She swiped her moist hands down the sides of her jeans. When they'd talked on the phone the other day, her dad had seemed grateful she was coming, but was that only because he'd needed her help to keep camp running?

She'd know soon enough.

She spied her dad splitting firewood in front of her childhood log home. He stopped when he spotted her coming up the drive. He put down his axe and tugged off his work gloves.

At forty-eight, Dad now sported a light-gray beard and mustache. He removed his faded blue baseball cap, revealing a full head of dark hair, and rubbed his forehead against the sleeve of his flannel shirt. As her truck approached, he lifted a hand to wave.

She parked her truck next to his and turned off the engine. After releasing a breath and saying a quick *"Lord, help me"* prayer, she opened the door and slid out.

Her dad moseyed over to her. Before she could stop him, he pulled her into a tight embrace. "I'm glad you're home. Grandma should be here soon. Darlene stopped by this morning and brought chili and cornbread for dinner so we can celebrate Grandma's return—yours as well."

As much as she loved the thought of seeing Grandma and the promise of a dinner from Darlene, the only thing that would make tonight perfect would be an apology from her dad for his hurtful words.

He released his hold. "Your room is exactly as you left it. Need help with your bags?"

She gave him a tentative smile. "I've got it."

Suddenly, the skin around his eyes crinkled and his eyes misted. "You look so much like your mom."

Her body tensed.

The lines on his forehead softened. "It was meant as a compliment." He whipped his work gloves out of his back jeans pocket and pulled them on, then returned to the woodpile. "Go on and get settled. I'll be done working soon."

Sierra went around to the back of the truck and removed her luggage from the cargo bed, then strode through the front door of the large two-story log cabin and ascended the stairs to her room, which was, as her dad said, exactly as she'd left it. Her empty closet door was left ajar and her bed half made, reminding her of her hasty exit. Why hadn't her dad thought to tidy things up before she arrived? Was it his way of leaving her to pick up the pieces?

She set her luggage on the chair in the corner and opened a window to get rid of the stale air, then made quick work of sweeping the hardwood floors, dusting the furniture and replacing the bedding to make it presentable. Next, she emptied her suitcase, putting clothes in the dresser drawers and closet, and toiletries in the bathroom.

Peeking out the bedroom window, she spotted the axe leaning against the stump and her dad stacking the firewood. She used this opportunity to roam the rest of the house.

In the living room, a brightly colored knitted blanket was neatly folded across the back of the couch. A new painting graced the wall above the stone fireplace, and scented candles were strewn about the room.

Once in the kitchen, she noted wildflowers in a vase, and a perfectly hung dishtowel over the handle of the oven. Her dad had never cared about such things. Why now?

Sounds of her dad's footsteps coming up the front walk startled her.

Quickly, she opened the cabinet door to grab a glass for water, but was met with plates instead. Since when had her dad rearranged the kitchen? She closed the cabinet door as the front door opened and her dad stepped inside.

"What happened to our house? So many changes." Her words shot out before she could stop them.

"Makes it more homey, don't you think?" Dad removed his work boots at the door.

A strange feeling gripped her stomach. The house definitely had a woman's touch. Had Grandma changed things or was her dad seeing someone?

Dad avoided her gaze and walked into the kitchen. He retrieved a glass from the cabinet that used to house the plates and filled the cup with sweet tea from the refrigerator. He set the cup in front of her on the peninsula. "Would you like some?"

"Thank you." She picked up the glass and tasted the drink. There was a hint of mint in the sweet tea—like Darlene made. "You said Darlene brought dinner over this morning?"

Dad's cheeks grew pink. "Yes." He opened the cabinet door to retrieve another glass.

Did her dad have a thing for Darlene Rushmore? Was she the one who had redecorated the house?

Darlene was a middle-aged widow who'd lost her husband in a tragic hunting accident. Darlene's Country Kitchen opened exactly one year after his death to provide for the twin daughters he left behind. Now the girls were both married with kids of their own.

Sierra took another swig of the sweet tea. She couldn't imagine her dad dating anyone, and if he were, she'd let him do the telling. "So who's picking up Grandma from the hospital?"

Dad opened the refrigerator door. "It's a surprise. Someone else is joining us for dinner."

Someone else?

Was it Darlene? Or was her father trying to set her up with someone?

She wasn't ready to date. And she doubted her father would pick someone suitable for her.

Recently, Matt Reed, her best friend from college, had wanted to take their friendship in a romantic direction, but Sierra had made it clear to him that they were best as friends. Matt had since moved to New York, although they spoke on the phone often.

She glanced down at her jeans and casual T-shirt. "Do I need to change?"

"A dress to welcome Grandma home might be nice."

Changing her clothes would be a good excuse to hide out in her room until Grandma arrived. It beat trying to make small talk with her father. "I'll be upstairs. Knock on my door when Grandma gets here."

"Will do," Dad said.

Once she stood in front of her closet, Sierra chose a pale yellow dress, perfect for spring. It was casual enough to be comfortable, and yet the lace at the hem made it feel a bit dressy too.

After she put it on, she sat in front of a small mirror and applied a touch of makeup, and curled the ends of her long blonde hair. She felt a bit silly getting all dressed up for a chili and cornbread dinner, and yet seeing Grandma again was cause for celebration.

A knock sounded on her bedroom door. "Grandma's here," Dad called from the hallway. "You ready?"

"I'll be down in a minute," she called back, slipping into her wedged sandals.

As she descended the stairs, she heard a familiar male voice talking in hushed tones encouraging Grandma to get off her feet.

It couldn't be...

"I know you're a doctor and all, but I'm fine, really," Grandma said. "It feels good to stand."

Sierra hesitated at the base of the stairs before she turned the corner and came face to face with Eric Holden. *Her* Eric. Or the man she had once called hers.

But he looked different than she remembered. His dark brown hair was more styled, his clothing more tailored, his shoulders broader. But his smile and light blue eyes were the same. He was even more handsome, if that was possible.

"Sierra! It's so good to see you." He stepped closer and held his arms wide for a hug.

As much as she wanted to step inside his embrace, she couldn't bring herself to hug him. Hugging her father was one thing—he had enveloped her before she had a chance to get away. Embracing Eric Holden would be altogether different.

Besides, how could he act as if everything was fine between them? He had broken her heart.

"Hello, Eric." She couldn't help the sarcastic edge to her tone. "What brings you here?"

"He's the new town doctor. Haven't you heard?" Grandma asked.

No, she hadn't heard.

She scooted away from Eric and stood by Grandma, wrapping a protective arm around the petite woman's shoulders. "It's good to see you, Grandma," she said, her voice low.

"You too, dear." Grandma smiled up at her.

She returned the smile, then pinched her brows. "What happened to Doctor Walters?"

"Doctor Walters retired," Eric said, "but you'll get to see him this week. He'll be the doctor at camp."

Thank goodness. The last thing she needed was to spend the entire week with her ex-boyfriend. Her heart couldn't take it.

Dad entered the family room, breaking up the awkward conversation. "Dinner's ready."

"Is Darlene joining us?" Grandma asked, as if it were a common occurrence.

Dad shook his head. "Not tonight."

"Too bad. I like that woman." Grandma turned toward Sierra. "She's been so good for your father—"

Dad cleared his throat. "Let's eat."

"You sure you want me to join you?" Eric's eyes landed on Sierra.

Was he asking her for her permission? If so, she'd gladly send him home. Becoming the town doctor didn't make up for ghosting her in college.

"Of course we'd like you to join us," Dad said. "Come take a seat next to Sierra."

Subtle, Dad. Real subtle.

Once seated at the table, she avoided Eric's gaze and took small bites of her chili and cornbread, waiting for the right opportunity to slip away.

Halfway through dinner, Grandma said, "Dr. Holden, do you mind helping me get settled in my room? I'm feeling a nap coming on."

"Certainly." Eric stood and retrieved Grandma's cane for support.

As soon as the pair rounded the corner of the dining room, Sierra set down her spoon, excused herself, and bolted up the stairs.

She'd help clean the kitchen as soon as Eric was gone.

CHAPTER FOUR

The following morning, Eric poured himself a cup of coffee and descended his apartment stairs to his office, his mind drifting to last night and the awkward meeting with Sierra. Did he really think she would give him a hug, pick up where they left off, have a friendship once again? That was definitely not the case.

Once in his office, he plunked down in his desk chair.

He had a lot of ground to make up, that was for sure. On a positive note, he had noticed her wrestling with her feelings, so she might still have a soft spot for him somewhere.

He sipped his coffee and looked at the day's schedule. It was light, but that didn't mean it wouldn't be busy. More often than not, walk-ins filled up his time, and before he knew it, it was closing time.

The doorbell rang.

He took a quick sip of his coffee before moseying down the hallway and answering the door. Alyssa stood on the threshold. His sister-in-law was in the latter stage of her second trimester and it showed.

"Alyssa! So good to see you." He welcomed her inside and gave her a hug. "Here for your Camp Jacobs adventure?"

"Yes." The petite woman smiled, but then her brows knit together. "But what is this about you not coming?

David was hoping you'd keep an eye on me. You know how protective he is. And with him out of the country, he's more paranoid than ever."

"I will be there every chance I get, but I'm needed here. I do have patients, you know." He smirked.

"Why can't Doctor Waters take over? I'm sure the community would be happy to have him back for the week."

"Doctor *Walters,*" he corrected her, "has plenty of experience taking care of expectant mothers. You'll be fine with him at camp. I promise."

"That's to be determined. Personally, I'd feel more comfortable with you around."

"Thanks. I appreciate that, but that's not the consensus around here. I found out the pregnant women of this community are going to Pigeon Forge for medical care. For everyone's sake, Doctor Walters is the better choice at camp."

"I see . . . " She seemed to be hedging.

"Is there something else bothering you?"

"With David's unexpected deployment, it took a lot of convincing for me to come on my own. I'm still not sure about this."

"I've been to Camp Jacobs many times. You'll be surprised at how peaceful it is."

By her furrowed brows, she wasn't convinced.

He glanced at his watch. He had an hour and a half before his first patient arrived. "Want me to come with you? I can't stay long—my first patient arrives at ten—but I can make sure you're comfortable."

She set her hands on top of her belly. "You'd do that for me?"

"Yes, for you and David," he said.

"Thank you." She smiled.

"You can follow me there." He hung his white coat on the hook and raced upstairs to grab his keys.

It was a short ride. The large camp sign on the left side of the road made it obvious where to turn, but for someone who'd never been to Camp Jacobs it could be easy to miss if they weren't paying attention.

The sign.

His mouth curved at the memory of painting it with Sierra. He'd kissed her for the first time as they stood close to each other, paintbrushes in hand. Had she also thought of the kiss yesterday when she arrived at camp? He hoped so.

Alyssa followed him to the main office. He pulled his car into the first available spot, leaving Alyssa and the other guests to occupy the spaces closer to the entrance.

He cut the engine and strode over to Alyssa's Honda Accord. She popped the trunk, and he stared at the six-piece luggage set.

She gave him a sheepish grin. "Okay, I admit I packed too much, but I have everything I need—"

"And some things you don't." He teased, grabbing the largest piece of luggage, and pulling it toward the smaller building next to the main house.

"Don't make fun of a pregnant woman." She laughed with him. "We are way too emotional."

He opened the office door for Alyssa, and they went inside.

His heart quickened when he saw Sierra behind the front desk. She glanced up, her right brow hitching when she spotted them.

"Good morning. Checking in?" Sierra's voice warbled.

Alyssa joined him at the counter. "Yes. Alyssa Holden. My husband won't be joining me this week."

"Oh? What a shame." Sierra looked at him, then back at Alyssa.

Did she think *he* was Alyssa's husband? They did have the same last name. And at dinner last night her dad had mentioned how Dr. Walters would be at camp to take care of their guests.

Alyssa fingered a brochure on the counter. "So I'll be by myself. I hope that's okay. I know this is a couple's retreat, but it can't be helped. Duty calls. Right, Eric?" She bumped his shoulder.

"But I'll be here every chance I can get," he said, wondering if this charade made a difference to Sierra.

"That will be nice..." Sierra quickly turned to grab a key off the wall, then placed a brochure on the counter. "You'll be in the Beaver cabin. It's a short distance down the path on your right. Here's a map to show you. We have golf carts out front for all our guests. Please feel free to take one."

"David is going to be so jealous. He's always wanted to drive one of those." Alyssa's excitement was palpable.

"David?" Sierra's voice rose a notch.

"Yes, my husband—Eric's brother. Wasn't that sweet of Eric to help me check in?"

"You should see her luggage." He winked.

Sierra's eyes roamed between them, then settled on the stack of papers in front of her. She shuffled them needlessly. "Yes, very—"

The click of the front door interrupted their conversation.

Kevin Jacobs walked into the main office and went to stand beside his daughter. "Sierra, thank you for stepping in. Sorry I didn't have time to show you our new computer system." He booted up the computer, his fingers working the keyboard.

Sierra peered over her dad's shoulder, then pointed at the screen. "Alyssa Holden is here. Her husband, David, won't be able to make it."

Eric's shoulders relaxed. Did he hear relief in her tone?

"Sorry to hear that," Kevin said. "Eric, I'm also disappointed you won't be joining us this week. But with family here I know you'll come often."

Eric smiled at Sierra. "As often as I can."

The muscles in her pretty jaw clenched. She glanced at her cell phone. "Oh, look at the time. I need to get to the kitchen."

"See you around, Sierra. By the way, the camp sign still looks good, don't you think?"

Was that a smile tugging at the corner of her lips? If he tried real hard, he still could imagine the feel of them when he'd kissed her.

He turned toward Alyssa. "Should we get you settled?"

"Yes, please."

He and Alyssa walked out the door with luggage in tow toward the row of golf carts.

"This one has my name on it," Alyssa said. The small blue flag attached to the cart waved in the Tennessee breeze. "I think I'm having a boy."

"Are you waiting until your baby is born to find out?"

"Most definitely," Alyssa said. "I didn't want to know the gender without David. I'm hoping he's home for the birth so we can have that special moment together."

"Makes sense." He loaded her luggage on the back of the golf cart. "You driving or am I?"

"Definitely me," she said. "I'll have to drive it when you're not here, so I might as well start now."

As they climbed in and Alyssa started the engine, he spotted Sierra walking toward the camp's kitchen and dining hall. The years had been good to her. She'd grown into a beautiful woman with curves in all the right places. Her long blonde hair was light and sun streaked. Her hazel eyes still captivating.

Even though he didn't get the reception he'd wanted, Sierra was back in Tennessee. And whether she admitted it or not, she was home.

CHAPTER FIVE

Sierra moved about the camp kitchen as if she'd never left. It helped that Grandma had kept every spoon, bowl, and pot in the same place since Camp Jacobs opened its doors and greeted their first guest.

She stirred the meat sauce, her grandma's recipe, and added a touch more herbs and spices to make the spaghetti her own.

Dad came up beside her. "Smells good in here."

Her heart warmed at the rare compliment. "Thank you. Want a taste?" She scooped up a spoonful of sauce and handed it to him.

He blew on it, and then placed it into his mouth. "Hmm, good. But a bit spicier than Grandma's," he said, his brows furrowing.

Over the past year, she'd experimented with different blends of Italian spices, adding a bit more basil here, oregano there, until finally settling on a combination that pleased her palate.

Was her dad disappointed? Most likely, but he would have to get used to her way of cooking if this was going to work.

Dad left the kitchen to gather everyone for supper.

She grabbed a spoon and tasted the sauce. Delicious. Just the way she liked it. Hopefully the guests agreed.

The oven timer dinged.

She scrambled to the other side of the kitchen, snatched a pair of oven mitts, and removed the cookie sheets containing the pre-sliced garlic bread. After placing the garlic bread in the large basket, she took the salad out of the refrigerator, and set out the dinner buffet style along the open-windowed counter.

Her eyes roamed to the clock above the kitchen door. It was a few minutes before six. Perfect timing.

As the guests formed a line, she spotted Eric standing beside Alyssa. What was he doing here? It was hard enough seeing him last night and then again this morning. It hadn't helped that for a brief moment she'd thought Alyssa was his wife. Fact was, if Alyssa hadn't mentioned her husband, David, Sierra might still have thought the pair were married. Of course if Eric were married, it would have at least given her a reason why he'd stopped communicating.

Her thoughts were spiraling out of control.

Get it together, Sierra. She bolstered herself to feed the crowd.

Her father stood in front of the line and raised a hand to get everyone's attention. "I want to thank y'all for coming to camp this week. Doctor Walters had a surprise commitment this evening, but Dr. Eric Holden is here for supper and s'mores, and to take care of any medical needs that might arise. Now before any assumptions are made, I want to make it clear that Dr. Holden is Alyssa Holden's brother-in-law, not her husband." He made a show of smiling Sierra's way.

Her cheeks heated. *Way to embarrass me, Dad.*

He motioned to Eric. "Come on up to the front of the line so you can greet everyone."

Eric meandered to the front. He turned toward the guests. "Nice to meet y'all."

Groans and whispers rumbled through the crowd. Sierra couldn't hear what people were saying, but it seemed as though they were unhappy about something—or someone.

"If you don't mind me asking, how much experience do you have birthing babies?" By the woman's size, she appeared to be expecting twins.

"Enough for you to be able to enjoy your dinner." Eric straightened his spine and smiled.

"Remember folks, Doctor Walters is coming back. No need to fear," Dad said.

"But what if I need care tonight?" The woman crossed her arms over her ample bosom.

"Me too," said another.

Murmurs of agreement went down the line.

Eric tucked his hands into his pants pockets. "I am very capable to assist you, but if there's an emergency, Pigeon Forge is not far away. I can assure you will have the best medical care while you're here at camp."

The mention of Pigeon Forge seemed to ease the woman's fears. The other couples seemed to accept his answer as well.

Meanwhile, her spaghetti supper was getting cold.

She cleared her throat to catch her dad's attention.

"Let's have a word of prayer before we eat." Dad bowed his head, and everyone followed suit.

As much as she needed to work through her feelings about her father, she enjoyed listening to him give thanks and talk to God as if he were his best friend. Maybe there was hope for their relationship too. On the surface they appeared to be getting along, but they had a lot of work to do if their relationship would ever be back to the way it was before she left.

When the prayer ended, the guests formed a line, and she scrambled to place pasta, sauce, and a piece of bread on each plate. Thank goodness the guests were in charge of getting their own salad.

"Need some help?" Eric asked, leaning into the kitchen window.

Even though she desperately could use his help, she found herself declining his offer. "I've got it."

His eyes pleaded with her. "Please let me help you."

Would it hurt to let him help? Serving dinner would take half the time if he did.

"Okay," she said. "I'll dish the pasta, and you can add sauce and a piece of bread."

"You've got it." He ran behind the counter to join her and donned a pair of rubber gloves.

She lifted a brow. "You might want an apron. You wouldn't want to get sauce on that fancy Oxford shirt."

He glanced down. "Good idea. Where can I find one?"

"Second drawer on the left." She scooped some pasta onto a guest's plate.

Eric returned wearing her grandma's ruffled gingham apron.

If he wanted the guests to take him seriously, that might not be the way to do it. She stifled a laugh and handed him a plate of pasta.

For the next fifteen minutes, they worked side by side. A few times her hand brushed his, making her insides flutter, but she pretended it didn't happen and moved on.

While serving dinner, most of the campers complimented Dr. Holden for his willingness to jump in when needed. Showed his chutzpah in order to get the job done—even if he looked silly wearing her grandma's ruffled apron.

Silly. And adorable.

She snatched a rag and started cleaning.

"Oh no, you don't. You've got to eat first." Eric handed her a plate of spaghetti. "Afterward I'll help you clean."

"It's not like you haven't worked a full day. Go join Alyssa and enjoy your meal."

He peered around the counter. "Alyssa looks like she's already made a few new friends. She's laughing and seems to be having a great time. And to be honest, I'm not ready to join the group."

"And why's that?" She scooped up a mouthful of spaghetti.

"Because that woman's question is the reason I'm not at camp all week." Eric removed the apron and tossed it on the counter. "They don't trust me."

"They're just scared. It's a new adventure for these couples having their first baby—"

"Not just these couples. Those who live in Dove Creek as well. They all go to Pigeon Forge for medical care. Doctor Walters told me as much."

Her heart melted a bit, but she wouldn't allow herself to feel sorry for him. She was supposed to be mad at him. He'd broken her heart, and she didn't trust him not to do it again.

"Well, Grandma's apron seemed to do the trick. You're welcome to borrow it anytime."

He rolled his eyes. "Very funny."

She stared at his handsome face and into his light blue eyes. Ugh, why'd he have to be so cute? She needed him to get far away from her before she did or said something she'd regret.

"Now please get out of my kitchen. I have work to do."

Confusion etched his face, but he didn't argue. Instead, he took his plate of food and joined Alyssa in the dining hall.

Somehow she felt worse than before.

Why did Eric have to move to Dove Creek and complicate her life?

CHAPTER SIX

At six o'clock the following morning, Eric sat opposite Dr. Walters in Darlene's Country Kitchen, a cup of coffee in his hands and an orange roll in front of him. "Are you sure Kevin is all right with that arrangement?"

"After the way you handled the women's heartburn incident last night, I'd say he's more than all right." Dr. Walters finished the last bite of his scrambled eggs.

"Sierra said she followed her grandma's recipe—although she admitted to adding more spices."

Dr. Walters sipped his coffee. "The bottom line is you've proved yourself a competent doctor."

All he did was suggest antacids. It wasn't as if he'd performed an emergency cesarean section.

"By the way, where were you last night?" There wasn't an ounce of accusation in Eric's tone. He tore off a section of orange roll and popped it into his mouth.

"My wife had something on the calendar long before I committed to being at camp. So when I heard you were available, I decided to make my wife happy."

Apparently it had worked in both their favors. Besides, the more time he spent at Camp Jacobs, the more he would see Sierra.

"So the remainder of the week, you'll keep an eye on my practice, and I'll work at Camp Jacobs?" Up until last week, that had been the plan all along. Why the sudden switch—again?

"That's the plan. All I need are your keys." Dr. Walters held out a hand.

Was he being paranoid, or did it seem as though Dr. Walters couldn't wait to get back to his former place of employment?

"Now, hold on." Eric kept his voice light. "Before I pack my bags I'll need to speak with Kevin. You sure that's what he wants? What the couples want?"

Why did he feel suspicious of Kevin and Dr. Walters's change of heart? His gut told him there was more to this story.

"Yes, Eric. I'm telling you the truth." The older man's eyes shifted to his coffee cup. He swirled his coffee around in circles, his gaze never wavering from the brew.

"By the way, the night nurse is off duty every morning at seven a.m. After last night's heartburn incident, it's best if you get there in time for breakfast." The doc said with a wink.

Eric downed the rest of his coffee and finished the last remaining bite of his orange roll. "I'll get the check and meet you out front." He headed toward the cashier before Dr. Walters could argue.

After Eric finished paying, he walked out into the cool, crisp air to join Dr. Walters. Eric took in a breath. Early morning was his favorite time of day. "Come to the office, and I'll show you around. I moved a few things." Why did he feel the need to explain? It was *his* office now, after all.

"No problem. See you there." Dr. Walters climbed into his Buick and drove the hundred yards while Eric walked.

It gave him a few minutes to think. If he'd known he was going to turn around and go back to camp, he wouldn't have left. Curiosity niggled at him. He still didn't understand why Kevin decided to bring him back.

He peeked at his phone—6:27 a.m. Would it be rude to call him now? As the director of a camp full of guests, it was likely he'd be awake.

He punched in Kevin's number.

After the third ring, it went to voicemail. Eric kicked at a stray pebble and left a message. "Hey, Kevin. Eric here. Just spoke with Dr. Walters. He said you wanted me to come to Camp Jacobs for the week. Can you please call me back to confirm? Thanks."

By the time Eric arrived at his office, Dr. Walters was standing by the front door.

Once inside, he showed the older man where he kept the prescription pads under lock and key, tongue depressors, and other miscellaneous items. The doctor harrumphed a few times, as if Eric's way of doing things wasn't up to the doctor's standards, but Eric pushed the grumbling thoughts out of his mind as they moved about the office.

"You'd better get along now." Dr. Walters all but shoved him up the stairs. "You don't have much time to pack."

"Yes, sir." He climbed up to his apartment. If he didn't know better, he would think the man was trying to get rid of him.

Simon greeted Eric at the door. He picked up the cat and scratched under his chin. "Hope Dr. Walters likes cats." He set Simon down, then placed a week's worth of cat food on the counter along with written instructions next to Simon's bowl.

Ten minutes later, he was packed and ready to go.

He grabbed a few protein bars and a water bottle on his way out the door, and carried his things downstairs. "Don't forget to feed my cat, Simon. And he likes his chin scratched, if you don't mind."

"Don't mind at all. Good luck, son." Dr. Walters smiled, his mustache twitching.

Good luck? The doctor didn't believe in luck. Neither did he. Divine appointment, providence, and hard work got people to where they needed to be. But he thanked Dr. Walters just the same as he walked out of the office with suitcase in tow toward his black Toyota Camry.

He arrived at camp a few minutes after seven. The door to the camp office was locked, so he headed to the medical station, a small cabin situated by the creek directly behind the camp office.

"There you are." A woman in her mid-forties looked him up and down, and by her wide eyes and sultry smile, approved of what she saw. "You are Dr. Holden, correct?"

It gave him a bit of comfort that his arrival wasn't a surprise. "I am."

"I'm Suzanne Keller, the night nurse."

He held out his hand. "Nice to meet you, Suzanne."

"If you don't mind, I'm going to grab breakfast in the dining hall. Would you like me to bring anything back for you before I leave?"

"No, thank you." He reached into his shirt pocket and pulled out a protein bar. "I've got everything I need."

"I'll be back in thirty minutes to collect my things."

"Take your time." He smiled.

A few minutes after the nurse left, Alyssa walked in. "You're here. I'm so glad it worked."

He raised a brow. "What worked?"

Her eyes brightened. "I'm the reason you're here."

"What's going on? Everything okay with you and baby?"

"Yes, silly." She sat on a chair and rubbed her belly. "I put two and two together during dinner last night. Sierra Jacobs is the girl you fell in love with all those years ago and the reason you moved to Dove Creek. And now, thanks to me and the other women who got heartburn last night, you are back at camp to rekindle your romance."

"Rekindle my..." Had he heard correctly? "So my return had nothing to do with my medical skills?" He brushed a hand through his hair.

"Don't get me wrong, you are a good doctor..."

Why hadn't her words felt like a compliment? "Thank you?" He set his hands on his hips.

"But every good doctor needs a supportive wife by his side." She giggled.

Wife? Sierra barely wanted to work beside him in the kitchen. "You mean friend."

"Yes, girlfriend." Alyssa pushed herself out of the chair. "Don't worry. The girls and I have a lot of ideas to help make that happen. Suzanne too."

His cheeks heated. So that was the reason for the nurse's perusal. "Thanks, but I'm capable of getting a woman all by myself." He held up a hand, agitation etching his tone. "May I remind you, you're here for a vacation, the last one before baby arrives. I'm here to focus on being your doctor—"

"Yes," she said with a wink. "And I have a feeling it's going to be a great week for all of us. See you around." She waddled out of the building.

If Alyssa and the other women followed through with their plan, this was going to make for a very interesting, albeit strange, week. Could he do it? Could he let the women help him win Sierra's heart?

The phone rang in the office. "Hello? Dr. Holden here."

"Eric?" Sierra's voice rose.

Were the ladies up to their shenanigans already?

CHAPTER SEVEN

"Sierra, what's wrong?" Eric gripped the back of his neck and gave it a squeeze. "Is Betty okay?" Normally he didn't jump to conclusions.

"Grandma's fine." Her words were pinched. "It's me. I feel so stupid, but I cut my finger on a kitchen knife. I can't stop the bleeding."

"I'll be there in a minute. In the meantime, cover it, elevate your finger, and apply pressure." As he gave directions, he gathered supplies.

"Okay. Hurry." Her voice squeaked. "I'm in the kitchen."

"And please sit down." He remembered Sierra wasn't too keen at the sight of blood. She'd nearly fainted when he'd scraped his elbow playing flag football that last year at summer camp.

"I'm already sitting down." Fear gripped her tone.

"Good. I'm on my way." He hung up the old-fashioned phone and grabbed his doctor's bag on his way out the door.

A few minutes later, he entered the camp's kitchen. He found Sierra sitting on the concrete floor, her back against the large refrigerator and her offending hand held high in the air.

The towel was stained crimson.

He knelt beside her. "Let me take a look."

She placed her hand in his and sucked in a breath as he slowly removed the towel.

Thankfully the cut on her left index finger was smaller than he'd anticipated, but it needed a few stitches.

As he debrided the area and placed a couple of sutures, he couldn't help but notice Sierra's eyes on him. Did she think he was doing a good job? Or was she wishing Dr. Walters was there to stitch her up? At any rate he was the one caring for her, and he was glad to help.

When he wrapped a bandage around her finger, a memory flashed through his mind about the first time he'd held her hand. He'd been so nervous. He'd rubbed his sweaty palm down the side of his jeans for the umpteenth time before getting up the courage to reach over and slip her delicate palm in his. As they walked around camp, their hands had swayed back and forth in time with their steps.

"Eric, are you finished?" Sierra's voice broke him free from his musings.

"Yes. All done." He smiled. "Keep the bandage clean and dry, and I'll check your finger in seven to ten days to see if the stitches are ready to come out."

Her brow furrowed. "How am I supposed to keep it clean and dry working in a kitchen?"

"It will be tough—nearly impossible if you ask me." He pressed his lips together. "Speak with your dad. He'll need to figure something out."

She scrunched up her nose. "Dad and I aren't speaking much these days." She covered her mouth with her bandage-free hand, as if she'd divulged a secret.

If only she knew the rift between them was old news in this small town.

An idea came to mind. "I hear Darlene hired a new chef, maybe she can help."

"Darlene? You mean the woman who rearranged our house and has eyes on my father?" She sighed. "No, thanks."

"You've got it all wrong." He lowered his voice. "Your dad has been pursuing her. He's been lonely without you around." He hadn't meant for his words to sound like a guilt trip.

She shrugged a shoulder. "Grandma's still here."

"True. But don't you think your dad deserves some happiness? He sure lights up whenever Darlene enters a room."

Sierra let out a breath. "Are you sure I can't run the kitchen by myself?"

"Not if you want your finger to heal. It's not worth getting an infection. Doctor's orders." He winked.

She nudged his shoulder. "You've always wanted to say that, haven't you?"

He laughed.

"Well, you can stop laughing and put on Grandma's apron. Breakfast is not going to serve itself." She gave him a pointed look.

"Is that so?" he bantered.

"Yes," she said, getting to her feet. "I've already boiled eggs and baked blueberry muffins for those who want a quick breakfast, but I'll need you to finish cooking the sausage before everyone else arrives. Oh, and I'll also need you to finish dicing the vegetables for the veggie platter I was making for this afternoon's picnic lunch. Everyone is going down to the lake. You should come."

Was she personally inviting him?

"You know, in case one of the pregnant women needs you." Her cheeks turned an adorable shade of pink. "Now that you've fixed my finger, I can totally vouch for you, unless you say something silly like 'Doctor's orders!'"

"Silly, huh?" He looped the ruffled apron over his head and glanced inside the skillet, seeing half-cooked sausage rounds. At least Sierra had the foresight to turn off the burner. He turned up the flame. "If only people followed their doctor's orders, they'd be a lot better off."

"Okay, okay. I'll be good, as long as people are willing to help." She sent him a cheesy smile.

"When you say *people*, you mean me." He directed a spatula at himself.

"If the shoe fits, or should I say apron?" She stepped behind him and tied the apron strings around his waist.

"As long as no one needs a doctor, you can count on me. Anything for my cute patient." He inwardly cringed. Talk about awkward. It was hard to keep things professional with someone like Sierra. They had a lot of history together—and yet, if it were up to him, not enough.

She ignored his comment and moved about the kitchen, using only her right hand. Truthfully, she should take the rest of the day off. A picnic lunch along the lake would be the perfect respite.

He turned the sausage. Even without an invite, he would have suggested he join the couples at the lake. It wasn't far, less than a mile, but far enough to save time if someone needed medical help.

Sierra added bananas and apples to the half-filled basket and placed it next to the eggs and muffins. "How's the sausage coming along?"

He flipped them over once again. "Almost ready."

She set a platter next to him on the counter. "Better hurry. They're coming."

The hum of people's chatter grew, and a line started to form.

He scooped up the sausage rounds and set them on the platter. "Here you go, boss."

"I like the sound of that." Sierra grinned, placing a serving fork on the plate. "You can put them on the end, next to the muffins. It's self-serve for breakfast."

Couples went through the line, dishing up their choices.

Sierra walked to the far end of the kitchen, sorting food into picnic baskets.

Alyssa and two other women came up to the counter. "There he is," said a woman he had yet to meet.

"Eric, I mean Dr. Holden," Alyssa said playfully, "my new friends and I were hoping you would come to the lake today." Her eyes darted to Sierra.

He could see right through her. "Is that right?" He placed a hand on his aproned hip.

"Yes." Alyssa rubbed her belly. "I've been feeling a lot of Braxton-Hicks contractions, and it would put my mind at ease if you came along. You know, just in case." She suppressed a smile.

The other women giggled.

He wouldn't joke about anything medically related. "Well, I'm one step ahead of you. Sierra already invited me."

The women's eyes lit up.

"She did?" Alyssa wiggled her brows.

"Yes," he said, pointing Sierra's direction. "As you can see by her bandaged finger, she'll need my help."

Alyssa's head tilted. "Your help, huh?"

He smirked. "Enjoy your breakfast, ladies, and I'll see you at the lake."

So far he hadn't needed the women to arrange time with Sierra. She was doing it all on her own. And he'd take any chance he could get—cut finger and all.

"Eric, those vegetables aren't going to chop themselves," she called from the other side of the kitchen.

She definitely enjoyed bossing him around.

Was it her way of getting back at him for his past mistakes?

CHAPTER EIGHT

Sierra opened her bedroom nightstand drawer and pulled out her journal from when she was a teenager. Dare she read it?

Today's finger injury and trip to the lake showed a side of Eric she hadn't seen before—one of doctor. He'd sweetly held her hand in his as he'd examined her finger, added sutures, and dressed her wound. Then while at the lake, he'd tended to a woman who was expecting twins, dehydrated, and needing fluids. Had he been as thoughtful as a teenager?

Sierra thumbed through the pages of her journal.

An extra blanket given to a camper.

Helping a friend while playing flag football.

Stopping by the camp's kitchen to thank Grandma for a meal.

Anyone could do those things, but Eric actually took the time and effort. And they must have made an impression because she had written them all down.

Then why would a caring guy like that suddenly end their relationship? The thought stung.

"Sierra," Dad called from the bottom of the stairs. "You going to the camp-sing tonight?"

Did she want to join the expectant couples around a cozy campfire? She could name many reasons why she'd rather stay home. Kids at camp had told her on multiple occasions that she couldn't hold a tune. And being a third wheel wasn't her idea of fun.

A rapping sounded on her door. "Sierra? We're having foil-baked apples—your favorite."

Her mouth watered. The cored apples filled with granola and cinnamon, and topped with vanilla ice cream were always a special treat. She tucked the journal back inside the nightstand drawer, then hopped off her bed and opened her door, facing her father. "Can you bring one home for me?"

"I can't make any promises," Dad said. "You know how fast they go. Please, come. Darlene is hosting tonight's event." A hint of a smile flickered on his lips.

Darlene.

Despite her and her father's differences, a protective feeling gripped her gut. Her brows furrowed and she crossed her arms. "Why do you care so much for Darlene?"

"Darlene has been such a godsend this past year. She's a good listener and really easy to talk to. I'd like to tell you more, but right now I need to meet her in the camp's kitchen. If you change your mind about the camp-sing, it starts in an hour." He turned to leave.

Eric's earlier advice rang in her ears. "Dad?"

"What is it, Sweet Pea?"

She sucked in a breath at the use of her childhood nickname. "Can you ask Darlene if she knows someone who can help me in the kitchen? Just while my finger heals . . ."

"I sure can." Dad rubbed his nose, a sure sign he knew something.

She released an audible sigh. "Did Eric talk with you already?"

"Who me?" Dad feigned innocence.

She rolled her eyes. "Honestly, can anyone mind their own business around here?"

"Not in this small town. And not when someone cares about you —"

"You'd better get going. You don't want to keep Darlene waiting." She regretted her snarky tone. Or did she?

Dad seemed not to care by the grin tipping up the corners of his mouth. "You're right about that."

Why was her dad being so sweet? She had yet to give him one chance to make things up to her. In fact, while he'd been kind, she'd been going out of her way to avoid a chance at reconciliation.

Eric's words ricocheted in her head. *Don't you think your dad deserves some happiness? He sure lights up whenever Darlene enters a room.*

It might be worth going to the camp-sing to see firsthand how Dad and Darlene got along.

As her dad descended the stairs, she called, "I'll see you at the fire pit."

"Great! See you then." The front door clicked shut.

After making sure Grandma was comfortable in front of the television with a blanket draped across her lap and a cup of warm tea in her hands, Sierra went to her room to add an extra layer and grab a jacket.

The last few days in Dove Creek had been unseasonably warm, but she didn't want to take any chances. Warm weather was one of the main reasons she'd driven out to California to start Plant and Go, but if she were honest with herself, she'd missed the cool Tennessee air.

On her way out the door she nearly bumped into Eric. She hadn't stood this close to him since they won the camp's square dance competition when they were teenagers. He smelled good and looked irritatingly handsome in his flannel shirt.

"What are you doing here?" Her words sounded like an accusation.

"Checking in on my favorite patient," he said.

She held up her bandaged finger. "Well, as you can see, I'm fine." She really had to learn how to soften her tone when it came to Eric. He was only doing his job.

"Actually, I'm here to see Betty."

Her face heated. "Grandma? I was just with her. She seemed fine and didn't mention you were coming."

"Mind if I check on her?" he asked.

"Don't mind at all. Come on in." She stepped aside and let him enter.

"You going somewhere?"

"To the camp-sing. Dad asked and I agreed." She shrugged.

Eric unzipped his jacket and set it on the stair rail. "That's a step in the right direction."

A step in the right direction? Did everyone know of the tension between her and her father?

"Hey, want some company at the camp-sing? I shouldn't be long."

She hesitated. It would be nice to sit beside someone. But did she want that someone to be Eric?

"I promise, I won't bite," he teased.

"Fine. I'll wait for you on the porch." She stepped outside and took a seat on the porch swing, her mind whirling at his invitation.

Five minutes later, Eric reappeared. "Ready to go?"

"Everything okay with Grandma?"

A grin spread across his face. "Yes, everything's fine."

"Why do I get the feeling Grandma planned this?" She wagged her hand between them. "The two of us heading to the camp-sing together."

He wrinkled his nose playfully. "She did mention it."

"I can only imagine what everyone else will say when we arrive."

"Does that bother you?"

Did it? How could she know when she barely had time to consider her own feelings in the matter? Most likely this was a big mistake. And yet, it wasn't as if this was a date. It was a group camp-sing.

They walked next to each other down the lit path as they'd done countless times before. But this time was different. They had grown up and grown apart. And as much as she'd like to pretend everything was fine, it wasn't. She couldn't trust that Eric wouldn't break her heart again.

The only problem? She'd never stopped loving him. And walking next to him now brought back all those feelings. How could she get out of the camp-sing without making things even more awkward between them?

His cell phone pinged in his pocket.

Eric pulled out the phone and checked the screen. "I'm sorry, Sierra. Looks like I'm needed at the office."

Relief surged through her. "No problem. I'll see you later."

At the fork in the path, they went their separate ways.

Would her heart ever beat a normal rhythm when it came to Dove Creek's newest doctor?

CHAPTER NINE

"Let me unlock the door, and then we'll check you out," Eric said to Alyssa, who clearly seemed upset, judging by the way her hands fidgeted in the glow of the outside light.

"It's probably nothing, but the Braxton-Hicks contractions seem to be getting worse," she said.

"How often is it happening?" He put the key into the lock and opened the door to the camp's medical office.

"At least a few times a day."

He flicked on the light and jumped when it revealed Alyssa's new friends gathered in the foyer. "What's going on?"

Alyssa giggled. "You, my dear brother-in-law, have been duped."

He ran a hand through his hair. "How in the world did you ladies get in the office?"

Suzanne, his nurse, walked into the room. "I let them in."

"We're here to kidnap you and take you to the camp-sing." Alyssa clapped her hands together. "A little bird told me Sierra would be there."

He folded his arms across his chest. "Okay, let's get one thing straight. You are not to use medical issues to manipulate me."

Alyssa bit her lower lip. "Sorry about that. From now on, no false pregnancy complications. I promise."

"It's my fault," Suzanne said. "I know better and shouldn't have agreed to their plan. But you need to loosen up and have some fun. Have you ever been to camp?"

Had he ever … if only his nurse knew he'd been to camp at least a half-dozen times.

"And secondly," he continued, "I was with Sierra only a few minutes ago. We were on our way to the fire pit when you texted."

"Really? That's great news!" Alyssa said.

"Not really. She was afraid of what you all would say if we showed up together. I think she's on to you."

"Hey, gals…" Alyssa herded her friends toward the door. "I'd like to speak with Eric in private, if y'all don't mind."

Suzanne opened the door. "Come on, girls. Let's go to the camp-sing."

When the women left, Alyssa sat on one of the waiting room chairs and patted the seat beside her.

He lowered himself next to her and with elbows on knees, clasped his hands together. "It's sweet of you to try and help me out in the romance department, but I'd rather do this on my own, in my own way—"

"I can tell you and Sierra have a history together by the way you banter. I have a good feeling you'll find your way back to each other." She gave him a sisterly pat on the back.

Eric hoped that was the case.

"You sure you don't need me to check on the baby?" he asked.

"I'm fine, really," Alyssa said. "And I'm sorry I called you here on false pretenses."

"All's forgiven." He stood and held out a hand to help Alyssa up. "Now let's go to the camp-sing."

When they arrived at the fire pit, Katelyn, a woman who still battled morning sickness, said, "Sierra, look who's here."

Sierra glanced up at him with a smile that didn't quite reach her eyes. "Hi, Eric. Hi, Alyssa."

"Mind if we sit here?" Alyssa pointed to the empty space beside her.

She scooted a bit to give them more room.

Alyssa sat beside Sierra.

"Would you ladies like hot chocolate?" Eric offered.

Sierra licked her lips. "Sure. Thanks."

"None for me," Alyssa said. "Chocolate keeps me up at night."

By the time he returned with two steaming mugs, his sister-in-law was gone.

He handed Sierra a cup and sat down. "Where'd Alyssa go?"

Sierra shrugged. "She said she was tired and wanted to go to bed early."

Katelyn sat directly across from them and wiggled her brows.

He had yet to give the other women the memo...no more trying to set him up with Sierra. Grandma Betty, however, was a different story. He'd let her orchestrate to her heart's content.

"Thank you all for joining us this evening." Kevin Jacobs stood in front of the crowd. "I want to personally thank Darlene for organizing tonight's event." He led everyone in a round of applause.